P9-CAD-105

There are many versions of this classic tale. In the tradition of the storyteller, each one is uniquely different.

Library of Congress Cataloging-in-Publication Data

José, Eduard.
  [Ali Baba y los 40 ladrones.   English]
  Ali Baba and the 40 thieves / illustration, Francesc Rovira ; adaptation, Eduard José ; retold by Janet Riehecky.
     p. cm. — (A Classic tale)
  Translation of: Ali Baba y los 40 ladrones.
  At head of title: From "The Arabian nights."
  Summary: A poor water-carrier discovers the well-hidden treasure belonging to a band of thieves.
  ISBN 0-89565-485-7
  [1. Fairy tales.   2. Folklore, Arab.]
I. Rovira, Francesc, ill.   II. Riehecky, Janet, 1953- .   III. Title.   IV. Title: Ali Baba and the forty thieves.   V. Series.
PZ8.J747Ali   1988
398.2'2 — dc19
[E]   88-36871
                           CIP
© 1988 Parramón Ediciones, S.A.   AC
Printed in Spain
© Alexander Publishers' Marketing and The Child's World, Inc.: English edition, 1988.

FROM "THE ARABIAN NIGHTS"

Ali Baba and the 40 Thieves

Illustration: Francesc Rovira
Adaptation: Eduard José

Retold by Janet Riehecky

The Child's World, Inc.

Once upon a time in far-off Arabia, there lived a poor water-carrier named Ali Baba. Ali Baba lived in a small house with his wife, Zoraida. The land around them was desert, so water was hard to find.

Ali Baba's job was selling water. Every morning Ali Baba loaded empty jars onto his mule and walked four miles to a nearby oasis. At the oasis he filled his jars with fresh water. Then he went out into the desert and sold the water to travelers. He only earned a few coins doing this, but it was enough money to live on.

One evening, on his way home, Ali Baba saw
forty men on horses, galloping across the dunes.
The men looked very fierce and carried spears
and knives and swords.

Ali Baba was curious about them, so he followed their tracks, staying far enough behind so that he wouldn't be seen. From the looks of them, Ali Baba suspected they were bandits.

Ali Baba followed for a few miles. Then he saw something that amazed him. The band stopped in front of a mountain. In the side of the mountain was a huge stone. Ali Baba hid behind a palm tree and watched the leader of the band approach the huge stone. The leader called out some strange words: "Open, Sesame!"

Instantly the huge stone rolled aside! Behind it was an opening into a cave. The forty men went inside and stayed for a long time. When they finally came out, the same man who had spoken before shouted, "Close, Sesame!"

And the huge stone returned to its place, covering the entrance. As soon as it was closed, the forty men galloped off, leaving behind a thick cloud of sand.

When Ali Baba was sure that he was alone, he approached the huge stone carefully. He wished to try the magic himself, so he said, rather timidly, "Open, Sesame."

It worked! The huge stone slid aside at the
sound of the words! Ali Baba entered the cave.
When he saw what was there, he almost fainted.
There were dozens of chests full of jewels, gold
coins, necklaces, and bracelets. Diamonds, rubies,
and emeralds were scattered in piles.

"Now I am sure those men are thieves!" said
Ali Baba to himself.

Ali Baba knew he had to leave quickly, but before he left, he loaded his mule with as much of the stolen treasure as he could carry. Then he slipped from the cave and shouted, "Close, Sesame!"

Ali Baba's wife greeted him with joy. All that treasure would take care of them for years! They hid most of the money and spent the rest carefully. They didn't want anyone to suspect that they had suddenly become rich, because they didn't want the bandits to learn who had taken their gold.

Ali Baba told the whole story to only one person besides his wife—his brother, Yusef. When Yusef heard the story, he wanted to get the rest of the treasure for himself. Ali Baba warned him to be careful, but Yusef was too greedy to listen.

Yusef collected six mules and set off for the mountain cave. He had no trouble finding it or using the magic words to open the door. Inside the cave, he was dazzled by all the treasure. Quickly he loaded all six mules, but there was still much treasure left! Yusef began replacing some of the items packed already on the mules. Every time he found something that was more expensive than what he had taken, he moved everything around. He changed one object for another and then another and then another, until . . .

"What are you doing here?" shouted a fierce voice behind him.

The bandits had returned unexpectedly and caught Yusef red-handed!

"You'll pay for this with your life," said their leader. And the bandits killed poor Yusef. Then they left his body and the mules in the cave while they went out to rob some passing travelers.

When his brother did not return, Ali Baba guessed what had happened. The next day he went to the cave. And, indeed, after he opened the cave with the magic words, he found the body of his poor brother lying on a pile of gold coins.

Weeping for his brother, Ali Baba buried him beneath a palm tree. Then he looked at the six mules loaded with treasure. It would be stupid to leave them behind, so he took them home with him. With all this money, Ali Baba bought a new house and helped all his relatives.

Ali Baba used his fortune to help many people. As time went by, he became known far and wide as a kind and generous man. But the leader of the bandits heard about Ali Baba and his sudden wealth.

"This must be the man who robbed us!" he told his followers. "We will have to teach him a lesson."

The leader of the bandits had a plan. He made forty huge jars, each big enough to hold a man. Then he ordered each of his men to get into a jar. The last jar was filled with oil. Then the bandit leader loaded the jars on mules and headed for Ali Baba's house. Disguised as a merchant, he knocked on Ali Baba's gate.

When Ali Baba greeted him, the leader of the bandits smiled slyly and said, "I have heard of your unselfishness, good Ali Baba, and I would like to ask a favor of you. I would like to spend the night at your house, so I may continue my journey tomorrow, feeling rested and refreshed."

"Yes, of course, my good friend," answered Ali Baba. He never guessed who the false merchant really was. "Come into my house. You can leave all those jars in the courtyard. What are you carrying in them?"

"The finest oil. I'm going to sell it in Marrakech," lied the bandit leader.

Later, while Ali Baba and the bandit leader were eating dinner, Zoraida, Ali Baba's wife, noticed that she needed a little more oil to finish the meal. She thought a moment and then decided no one would notice if she took a little from the merchant's jars. She went down to the courtyard and knocked on one of the jars to see if it was full. To her amazement, a muffled voice came from inside the container.

"Is it time yet?"

Zoraida was frightened, but she kept her head. She answered, "Not yet."

The brave woman checked each of the other jars. And at all but one the same thing happened. Zoraida would knock and a man's voice would ask, "Is it time yet?"

Then Zoraida would reply, "Not yet."

After Zoraida checked all forty jars, she hurried to the guards and told them what she suspected: terrible thieves, wanted by the police, were hiding in thirty-nine of the jars. The guards came and surrounded the jars, ready to capture the thieves.

Meanwhile, Zoraida went back to the dining room. Ali Baba and the false merchant were having a friendly chat.

"I may decide to ask you for some oil next winter," said Ali Baba.

"I would be happy to sell you oil," said the false merchant. "You will see that there is no finer oil than the oil I sell."

"It must be fine," said Zoraida. "It can even talk."

Ali Baba stared at his wife, wondering what she was talking about. But the bandit leader jumped to his feet, knowing his men had been discovered. He started to attack Ali Baba, but two guards rushed in. The bandit leader fought hard. He had been in many fights and was very strong. Finally, though, he was defeated. The thieves hidden in the jars were also captured, and all forty bandits were taken before the judge. He ordered them imprisoned for life for their many crimes.

Ali Baba told his whole story to the caliph, who was the ruler of the city. The caliph ordered most of the treasure to be returned to its owners. The treasure that couldn't be returned was divided between Ali Baba and the caliph.

The huge stone covering the entrance to the cave was broken into a thousand pieces. But to this day travelers still stop there, for there is still magic in the cave. When the caliph's guards took away the treasure chests, a magical stream of crystal clear water sprang up from the ground. The water was beautiful, cool, and refreshing. And in the desert, fresh water is the greatest treasure of all!

6/2003- C\/C (37)
* Reclassed from E RIE